WAKE

a novella

Michael Spinelli

DEDICATION

For my wife,
who always believes in me and why? I sometimes never know.
My baby and my baby mama.
This one is just for you.

Wake

CONTENTS

ACKNOWLEDGMENTS

To my two boys, who make me want to be a better human being every day.

To my Mom and Dad, for without either of whom, I could not be here.

To my pal Rube, who has read and listened.

To anybody else that has ever taken the time to read any of my raving nonsense.

Author's Note

This story is NOT for the faint of heart.

Don't say I didn't warn you.

Mike Spinelli
July 2017

CHAPTER 1:

TWO MEN AND A BOAT

It was dark and the two men and the boat were already a good distance out to sea. The boat motored along at an even if slightly lumpy pace, feeling the predawn tide thump, thump, thumping along the hull.

The scruff looking man powering the boat was cold, but he was ignoring that right now. There was extreme fun to be had up ahead and cold be damned.

The other man lay unconscious in the bottom of this glorified tin dingy with an engine. His hands and ankles were zip tied behind him and while he slept, he dreamed. The sound of the waves crashing against the side of the craft and the salty ocean air brought events back up from his pre-teen subconscious and made his dreams bad.

And here he was. Indeed lying unconscious in a not so big boat, heading further and further out to sea with a very mad man at the wheel. Oh, how upset he was going to be when he would wake. So upset.

The man above him, steadfast and with purpose, powered on. Constantly checking for that glow between the ocean and the sky that signified the approaching dawn. He looked again, but still nothing. There was some small amount of time left before he arrived at his destination, but he was getting close. He could feel it. How many times had he come out here like this, spilling blood? Most certainly, he was bloodthirsty tonight, not that you would know by the look of him. The man behind the wheel was calm as a dead Buddhist monk on Thorazine, which is to say, passive.

The man at the bottom of the boat was starting to stir. The up and down thud, thud, thud coming from the boat, speeding through small wave after wave, was bringing him around. He moaned loud. Mr. Bus driver hit the brakes some and the boat began to slow. The wind, while certainly still blowing, calmed a bit. The incessant bumping and thudding that had been ongoing for some time became a deep purr of the engine. Now, it was just that and water getting out of the way of the broad bow of the boat. The man stirred again, wincing in pain. He was coming too, face down and his head was throbbing. He was bound wrist and ankle, cold and soaking wet on top of it all. Needless to say, he was confused.

He looked up at the man across from him and the man stared right back. There was no give in that face. He knew now that he should probably be scared and not just simply confused. He just didn't know why yet and that seemed to move him from the category of "should probably be scared" to just plain old scared.

He was shaking all over. At first it was just from being cold and wet and soon after, from everything else. He used what little leverage he could muster from the position of his legs to hoist himself up, his back against the metal bench in the middle of the boat. In a way it was funny. Despite the cold. Despite the wet. Despite the sound of the engine and the up and down repeated thuds and bumps that signify the look, feel and sound, of a boat moving through the water. Despite all of that, the man in the bottom of the boat left behind what he would soon realize were actually sweet dreams he was having for sheer terror, when he realized precisely where he was.

He started taking long, panicked breaths.

He tried to say, "Where am I?" but it came out with a stutter and garbled.

Nothing.

The man stared straight ahead and said nothing.

"Please!" he begged. "Where…where am I? ", he choked, then coughed.

Nothing still.

More and more frightened, he lashed out. "TALK TO ME!"

The look on the rugged man's face driving the boat suggested he sensed defiance and a demand. He flashed a look, which if looks could kill, would have caused instant death. The look was nasty enough to immediately gain the silence that it had been seeking.

The dark was still the dark and not much anything else could be seen except the dull shimmy of their immediate surroundings. A new moon was nearly upon the earth and only a sliver of silver remained, casting the faintest of flashlights on their own private spot in the sea.

The once screaming man, who had moments earlier laid an unwise demand upon a man he did not know or understand, but feared, realized this was not the approach he should be taking here. He took a moment to try and slow his still racing and panicked heart and mind. He took a quick stock of inventory on his current situation. It was not looking good.

He was on the water. Somewhere, with someone. And he knew absolutely jack shit about either of those two things in particular. All he knew beyond that were that his hands and feet felt useless to him and he had a massive fucking headache.

He breathed in slow and deep.

"Sir?" the man in the bottom of the boat spoke softly. He repeated and augmented, but softly still. "Sir. How did I get here?"

The man driving the boat glanced his way. Much slower than the last turn of his head, but still no softer in his gaze.

"Ask", the dark pilot thought to himself, "and ye shall receive."

CHAPTER 2:

SHOPPING

The same scruff, rugged man who only a few hours from now would be powering a boat out to sea at a decent speed, was at this very moment sitting at the wheel of an entirely different vehicle altogether.

He sat in a relatively late model Japanese car. He would never answer directly when asked what car he drove. These goddamn Japanese cars made him afraid of being ridiculed when he would invariably mispronounce it. He would just say foreign. He had heard somebody at the dealership remark that the vehicle's name was pronounced like Sunday, but he thought that person might have been, in His estimation, a retard. He knew people didn't like that word any more these days, but when he grew up it was rampant and used for just about anything in the world of insults. But it was his go to word for forty years. What was he to do?

"No, the hell with that," he thought. "Foreign car it is and forever it shall be."

He sat there behind that wheel waiting. Waiting for someone to come on out of that grocery store. The right someone. Plenty of people had come waltzing in and out of there for the last forty minutes or so. Just not the right person. He had started to wonder if he had missed him, but the man's car was still parked where it had been when it had first arrived nearly an hour ago. But he was patient. His patience would outweigh his panic, as it always did and tonight, as in most nights, it would pay off here. Just a few moments later a man emerged alone, cart chock full of groceries and bags.

The man with the grocery cart full of breakfasts, lunches and dinners that would soon spoil, was a teacher. A Gym teacher, but a teacher nonetheless. He was well regarded by most of the staff and some of his students even. His name was James Flannigan Junior, or Jim Junior as his whole family had called him as far back as could be remembered. Jim Junior, the gym teacher, walked to his car with his cart, a red Volkswagen Beetle. He stepped to the trunk, pressed a button on his keychain, popping it open and began the tedious job of loading groceries from cart to car.

He managed to be one of the few people that still requested paper bags from his grocer, not plastic. He did his part to save the world when he could. He believed heavily in this global warming thing and the naturalistic theories regarding cause and effect. He was no scientist or even science teacher, but he certainly had his own opinions and he was gonna be goddamned if he was going to listen to some money hungry asshole deny it was happening.

He took the paper grocery bags out two at a time until he was done, climbed into the drivers seat and started the car. He looked cautiously both ways before slowly backing out of his parking space an inch at a time; until he was absolutely sure no one was coming and then drove off towards home. Completely oblivious and unaware that he was being watched and stalked. Clueless to the fact that here, in this very moment, he was a little pig in the company of the Big Bad Wolf.

The wolf drove a couple of cars back, keeping the little pig feeling all safe and cozy in his tiny house of straw.

Jim Junior only lived about ten miles from the store, so it did not take him too long for them both to reach their final destination.

The gym teacher parked, not noticing the other car that parked a mere twenty feet away. He turned the ignition to off and then removed the key and then himself, from the car. He walked casually around to the back, whistling and spinning his keys coolly around his left forefinger. He caught the key ring mid swing and nailed the trunk button with his thumb as the door popped open once more. Removing bags this time, he took out two at once stacking them in the crook of one arm as he snagged a third with the hand currently holding the keys. He took that now half full second hand and pushed the trunk closed. There were more packages still to get but he would key into the house and put these on the kitchen table and then return for the rest three at a time until the end. He hated leaving the trunk open with groceries or items of any kind and wanted to nail this in two trips not three. He didn't live in a bad neighborhood, "but why tempt fate?" He thought. Besides, he was exhausted. He was simply not in the mood. It had been a long day at school on top of a long month in general and he had had enough.

He was so tired in fact, that he did not see the beast crouched right there in the weeds. Waiting breathlessly, silently for his prey to resume drinking from the water hole. Jim Junior felt it for a moment, but did just like so many of us that have that gut feeling that we are being watched. And yet, at that key moment, when it matters most, we disregard it. We push it aside at our peril.

Jim Junior took the hand with the keys and only one paper bag clutched with the last three free fingers and tried to put the key into it's lock while balancing the other arm's two bags on his knee. It was quite the sight. It was then, just then, at Jim Junior's moment most awkward and vulnerable, that the wolf sprang from the dark brush and slammed the gym teacher, forehead first, into his really hard wooden door. Jim Junior fell straight to the ground in a heap of flesh and bone. The force from the impact sent groceries scattered in all directions inside and out of the house.

The darkly dressed man then took a small club from behind himself and added one more solid thud to the back of Jim Junior's crown, assuring he would sleep for some time.

He dragged the unconscious teachers body into the house all the way and slammed the door closed. No one on the street or in their homes knew or heard of anything. Once inside he bound him wrist and ankle and began the next steps of his oft-rehearsed plan.

Step One: He would find every suitcase in the house and fill it with every article of clothing leaving all things of value, jewelry, television, Blu-ray player, whatever. There must be absolutely NO sign of break in or robbery. None at all.

Step Two: Retrieve wallet and identification. Credit cards and any pertinent paperwork, files, thumb drives, all to be disposed of.

Step Three: Remove VIN number and license plates after abandoning car down by the pier. Keys in ignition, ready to be lifted by...whomever.

Step Four: Back to the house. Collect his Gym teacher and be on his way.

The severe looking man handles steps One and Two with ease. Step Three took some time, but time he had. He gave Jimbo a tranquilizer shot to the upper left ass cheek to guarantee his slumber in his stead. He drove the long thirty minutes to the docs and left it under a street lamp for all the criminal underworld and vagrants to see. Then, dressed dark as the night, he crept amongst the vast shadows of the bay. He walked nearly 3 miles before hopping a bus back to midtown and then traveling the remaining three miles back to the teachers digs on foot.

It was just about one in the morning and he was beginning to pick up the pace. Right now, time was on his side. But he knew. He KNEW that could always go south. Sometimes all your plan ever is, is a list of shit that doesn't happen. But that be damned too. He was going to do it or die trying. That's just who he was. Once the wolf had its prey in its mouth, there was no letting go. This was certainly to be no different.

He keyed back into the house and found the gym teacher to be snoozing right where he had left him. He loaded his truck with the suitcases, then he went back inside, still gloved and wiped down any thing he may have passed in his travels, even though he damn well knew he touched nothing. He had shaved his head; arms and legs clean the day before. He was a cautious man and he was quite aware that, when this one went missing, the world around him would notice. They would notice, and then they would come looking. As squeaky clean as he was leaving things, he knew someone would notice. And when they did, they would look for any and every goddamn hair, print, track, smudge, stain and fucking fiber that they could get their eyeballs and ultimately, hands on. When they had exhausted their efforts of finding evidence, they would begin the process of finding what evidence there wasn't.

He was careful when he had to be, and now, he knew he had to be.

He threw the teacher into the back of his vehicle, stopped to take one more complete look around. One more look to check for any faces or lights peering from random windows or hidden in shadow walkways. Holding his gaze and tilting his head to pick up any movement or sound he may have missed in his first sweep.
Nothing.

He closed the gate to the pickup and slipped into the driver's seat. He took the keys to the ignition and smiled angling his head towards his catch in the back. He turned the key and she turned over nice and easy. He pulled away, driving plus or minus 2 miles per hour around the speed limit. Making sure to come to a complete stop at EVERY stop sign, red light, crosswalk and or railroad track. With every turn, came a judicious use of the blinker for a solid one hundred feet before the turn.

He had been driving for nearly forty minutes and he was almost where he needed to be. He had begun to slow down, as he was fast approaching an intersection he knew whose light changed quickly. Sure as shit, he was fifty yards away and it went from green to red so fast. Its speed was as if it was with, a certain disdain for yellow. This traffic light was the last touch of normal dry land civilization before the isolated beachfront that lie just a few miles ahead. He sat in his vehicle quiet and still, waiting for the light to change back to green the way it had to red. No such luck. He kept looking in the rearview and was making himself paranoid. He couldn't see any lights, but he felt off. If he had had Spidey senses, this is where they would be tingling. He heard a "thunk" from behind himself in the bed of the truck. He looked over his shoulder to see his catch, still unconscious; snap it's legs out in a spasm of sorts and rock his head further into the side of the truck. He almost laughed, but something else caught his eye, just passed the height of the truck bed. It was a cyclist. Well what the Sam hell? he thought to himself . He asked the question and his mind, ever so kindly answered. He knew exactly what this was at two something in the AM. It was a goddamn cop on a bike. He was almost fifty yards away.

"You have got to be kidding?" he thought out loud to no one. Come on light. He kept looking from the light to the biker approaching casually. He needed to have this light change and now. If the cop got up close enough to see a plate, make, model or color he was fucked. There was no plan B. Would he kill the Cop? he wondered to himself, internally this time. Then, just as the answer was about to creep into his mind, his question was answered for him. The light flashed green and he stepped firm but gentle on the gas and got going. He watched the cop fade into blackness as he looped back, turning around after reaching the light. End of jurisdiction.

Five or so more miles down, the road became a series of turnoffs to the left. Heading down to the water, he pulled off on one particular path that he had recently made himself. His own little known spot. His entrance to the Gulf of Mexico. There wasn't a gas station for miles. There wasn't anything or anyone anymore, for that matter, especially at this time in the morning. The last life he had seen was left back with the bicycle cop over five miles ago. This was the beaten path OFF the beaten path.

Finally, there it was. He had cleared the tall grass and made it to a wet and sandy, small patch of beach. The dark, purposeful man threw the pick up in park and got out. His cheap but sturdy metal boat, tied off to a mangrove right where he had left it. He cleared past the brush. He thought to himself about he little near miss with the Schwinn Patrol that had rattled his cage for a moment, but only a moment. He was back to business and back on track, being that he was nearly at the finish and could not let up or relax now.

The boat was just big enough for two men and a few supplies, but small enough to mostly go unnoticed at this hour and in this light. He began to pack the boat with his prize with a capital P and some other small supplies. He semi gently dropped the teacher into the boat, clunking his head carelessly against the inside hull accompanied by a gong type noise. A small anchor, a large bucket, a life preserver and some rope, then he himself, joined the gym teacher. He was doing well; it was not quite three am yet. He had nearly three hours to go before sun up, and he had a ways to go and then the same to come back.

Not wasting any time, he untied the rope from the tree limbs and pushed off, floating out of grounds way. He waited about thirty seconds and then pull started the engine. As he crept slowly and silently out to sea, he waited until shore was just but a blur before he opened up the engine's throttle, to it's fullest, loudest potential.

It was dark and the two men and a boat were already a good distance out to see. The boat motored along at an even; if slightly bumpy pace, feeling the predawn tide thump, thump, thumping along the hull.

CHAPTER 3:

CLASS

The gym teacher lay there stunned and terrified. What miserable, shitty ass bullshit misfortune had befallen him this time? He found himself wondering. He had begun to remember moments from his day leading into his waking cold and wet and lying in this small metal boat. He had to think. He had to get a hold of himself and think. If he didn't think he was dead for sure. He just couldn't seem to get a hold on the last thing that happened before this. Think damn it, THINK! He yelled at himself. Yesterday morning. He remembered yesterday morning.

He had had his normal weekday preparation for school. He would jog, shower, dress and eat. Count Chocula and coffee, breakfast of champions. His first class didn't start until nine but he showed up at seven like the real teachers did. The "REAL" teachers… Hardy fucking har. That was the mentality around here amongst the other faculty. Not so much english and history. Those guys were on their own teams respectively and almost all encounters were cordial if not pleasant. But the math and science bimbo twins? They were the worst. They talked down to him at every turn but acted like nothing happened at all come lunch. One time, the math and science bitches were actually having a discussion of useless school programs and decided to lump him in that awesome subject with the art and music teacher. He would say, "misery loves company," but what company? The art teacher doubled as the goddam music teacher for Christ sake. It was like high school within a high school. Smile and wave boys, smile and wave.

This was his first day back from a two-week leave and things felt like they were just starting to get back to normal. Just a bit less than a month ago one of the quieter students named Brian Anderson, had committed suicide by hanging himself in his bedroom. It was tragic and wildly confusing to all. There were kids he disliked and some he liked more than others, but he never wished one dead. There was no answer as to why, as the boy, it seems had left no note to explain himself. The family held a small service and the school a large one. All students and teachers were in attendance and it was bad. Quite bad in fact, that some questioned whether there should have been anything at all. A lot of overwhelming grief and emotions. The boy had kept to himself, but was pleasant and well liked. Ironic that such a quiet and oft times unnoticed boy could be missed and his very departure felt by all.

Things were really rocky when the boy had first been found and the whole area aware of what had happened. It was pandemonium and Jim Junior had to get away. A few other teachers took leave for a week or so. Substitute teachers of the world rejoice. The boy, being so quiet and agreeable, was a favorite to some of the teachers. Students that calm and respectful don't come waltzing down the halls every day in high school, you know. That sort of demeanor was a rare commodity and they were qualities Jim Junior liked as well.

So, he left the madness for the Caribbean a bit until this all calmed down and the air cleared a little. And he felt, while walking down the halls, virtually unnoticed by the students, that it had. Kids talked when they roamed the halls before, after and between classes. If a teacher wanted to know all the latest and greatest of the juiciest tidbits of gossip, all one had to do was stand just outside the classroom door or just walk silently amongst them. You could get all one needed to know. Kids didn't notice adults anyway. Not unless they had done something stupid enough to garner their attention like accidentally set the backyard on fire or knocked their annoying kid sister down a flight of hard wooden steps. Nope…the teacher in Charlie Brown. Whaa whaa whaaaa. That was only Phase One of the gossip.

Phase Two: The Teachers. Phase Two was where all of the dirt was collected and compiled from all of the little snippets and morsels of dialogue that had been shoehorned and molded into one final story that either resembled, to one degree or another, the truth of what had happened or was the most insane piece of glorious steaming pile o'shit fiction you had ever heard. Most times though, it ended up being a truer closer look at what had happened.

Hundreds of kids talking for hundreds of hours over weeks and weeks seemed to form a pretty solid picture. Jim Junior, being gone for most of that, was able to hear a coherent story told in one long single take. Midway through his day he stopped in at the teachers lounge. Not much happening there and what was being talked about, was only less interesting retreads of the same news he had heard all morning long.

There was still heaviness in the air after nearly three weeks, but over time, as things always tend to do over time no matter how horrible or painful, things would get back to normal. He had five classes and a study hall today. Mondays. They were his fullest days and most despised.

He had arranged for the students to do rapid-fire team building exercises all day long. Exercises that did not require much of him. Anything at all if we are being honest with each other. He had rested in his time away from it all, but it was solitary and an uneasy rest. He felt he needed more, but there was no more time to take. He had used bereavement time when his mother passed in the beginning of the year and was sick around the holiday time off. There were no more tickets and there was no more train. After school this time of year, he was the boys Junior Varsity Volleyball Coach. That always got him a bit of ribbing from the likes of the football and lacrosse coaches. Hell, even the soccer coach gave him shit. Volleyball was what the boys did who couldn't make the cut on the tougher sports and felt the need to fulfill the requirements of a three-sport athlete.

Practice went until four thirty and then it was showers and then kids home and then, his quote, unquote teacher's paperwork began. Giving some of these kids' grades for gym class was comical. Top letter grades would depend on only a mere handful of items.

1. Dressing for Gym.
2. Participating in Gym.
3. Showering after Gym.

That third one was non negotiable. That was the one piece that could land you a D, because no one ever got an F. You had to miss seventy percent of your classes, not do any of the three big qualifiers AND tell the teacher to go fuck his dead mother, to get an F. An F in Gym would almost certainly be a major indicator of someone not advancing to the next grade.

Besides, he was running a weigh station here, not an assembly line that conveyer belts the pieces into a warehouse for storage. No. No, just a new batch of recruits' year after year. In one door and out another, no repeat business here, thank you very much.

His day had lasted about eleven hours from start to finish, but it may as well have been thirty, or so he had felt. By the time he had finished up completely it had become dark out. He followed rule number three, got dressed, climbed into his car and drove away home. He had nearly reached said destination when he had realized he had forgotten to stop at the Kash-N-Karry a few miles back the way he came, for some key essentials. He pulled a quick U-turn and headed to the grocery. He pulled into the semi-congested parking lot a few minutes later, parked, got out and went inside. It seemed unusually busy for this time on a Monday night. He grabbed a mini cart and stalked his goods, isle by isle, as he had also forgotten his list. Clearly NOT on his game today.

He turned down isle nineteen. It was a short dark isle near the back of the store, an island to itself of crappy about to go bad on sale candy and the like. There was a young teenaged boy at the end of the small isle with his back to Jim Junior. The boy was looking towards the opposite end of the isle, towards the front of the store as he gingerly stuffed his pants, jacket and socks with an assortment of candy bars, Tootsie Rolls and Skittles. The off duty gym teacher looked around in all directions to also make sure that no one was looking as he approached the boy stealth fully from behind. As the boy crammed the last piece of bendable candy into his tighty whities, Jim Junior, the gym teacher, reached out slowly and grabbed the top of the boy's left shoulder and gently spun the boy around to face him. Panicked, the boy jumped at this, spilling several pieces of candy all about the hard grocery store floor with a loud CLACK-CLACK-CLACK! sound.

The boy's face, now white as a sheet and mouth hanging agape, gasped. He sat there looking stupefied, gasp still held deep in his lungs, afraid to exhale, wondering just how busted he really was right now and by whom? This man, while not the tallest person in town, towered over him. Magnified by how small the boy was for his age, the boy shook. The man knelt down on one knee to the closest candy bar to the young boy's feet. He looked at the boy's still trembling face and then looked around once more to make sure they were still unseen. The kid watched this strange man look around to see the coast was clear in turn causing him to do the very same thing, but could not for the very life of him, figure out why. The man stood back up, towering over him yet again.

"Seriously kid?" James Junior asked rhetorically.

The kid, looked around to see if he was being filmed for some prank show and continued to stare as if the answer was still out there somewhere.

"You ready to go to jail over a Snickers bar? You know, you can see your clothes are jam packed with stolen goods from all the way on the other side of this store." Blank staring continues.

"Now", the teacher started softly, "empty all of your pockets."

The still speechless kid started to slowly get the idea that this was all really happening and started to move his hands accordingly. He slowly started emptying his coat and pants of it's contents but rather than extend his hand a bit and place the candy back on the shelf he got it from, he just started dropping it down on the hard floors making more than just a few small CLACKITY CLACK sounds. The sounds seemed to branch off into eternity and this time they both looked around simultaneously to see if anyone else had seen or heard.

Still, no one.

"All of it," Jim Junior insisted still soft but firm, "or I'll do it for you."

The boy gulped so hard he seemed to be attempting to swallow his Adam's apple for good, as he crashed his hands into his pockets again spilling candy and other assorted shit onto the floor once more.

"Now…" the teacher began softest yet and after a brief pause, "get the fuck out of here." The kid turned to run but seemed to be having a spot of trouble getting his feet to follow his upper half out the door. The kid took his first steps before Jim Junior grabbed after him, catching his elbow.

"Hey," he said calmly, "be smarter next time."

He released him and then the teen, who had been pulling in the direction of the exit the entire time he was being held up by this strange stranger by his elbow, nearly fell to the ground. He stopped himself from falling by mooshing up against the shelf holding the candy he had until recently, been trying to pilfer. As he hit the shelf it lightly rocked and more candy tumbled from it and clacked on the ground just enough to freak him out the rest of the way out of the store in the closest thing to a run walk that one could come up with.

Jim Junior gathered up the remaining candy from the floor in two giant handfuls and placed it back atop the shelf from whence it came. He smiled a slick smile to himself and started to push his more than half filled cart to the front of the store for checkout. He passed the end of isle ten and grabbed another box of Count Chocula as he was nearly out of that after this morning. He loved that cereal. Boo Berry was his absolute favorite as a kid, but he just couldn't find that one anymore. So, Count Chocula it was. He had clung to a great many of the staples of his childhood. In a lot of ways, he never really grew up.

The cereal was just another example of one of those things he could never seem to grow out of.

He checked out at the register with a salty old lady that worked there since the dawn of man, named Esther. She gave him her usual gruff questions and answers and sent him packing with nary a smile. He finished bagging his own paper bagged groceries and rolled his cart right out the front door and drifted across the black asphalt to his car, a red VW Bug, popped the trunk open and started loading his groceries from cart to car. He took the paper grocery bags out two at a time and placed them into the trunk until done. He climbed into the driver's seat and started the car. He looked cautiously both ways before slowly backing out, an inch at a time, until he was sure no one was coming and he drove off towards home. Completely oblivious and unaware that he was being watched and stalked. Clueless to the fact that here…here, he was the little pig in the company of the Big Bad Wolf.

CHAPTER FOUR:

MACHINATIONS

After running through a mental checklist of the events of his last "normal" day leading up to his abduction, he couldn't recall a single detail or clue as to who this maniac was or why this was happening to him.

After miles and miles of questions and yet not even one square foot of reply, he thought he would try again. Anything to reach the man, anything to stop what seemed to be inevitable at this point. Anything but drowning, he thought loudly to himself. ANYTHING. He was going to have to think and think hard and fast if he was going to weasel out of this one. He would try again.

"Sir." this was a statement not a question. "Sir, please. Don't do this." Jim Junior stared, desperate in the face of this man who refused to budge. He thought to say something like, "I have a little girl, don't drown me all the way out here. PLEEEEEAAASSSEEEE!!" and then thought better of it. If this man knew anything about him at all, he would know there was no fucking daughter. And just how much did this guy know about him anyway? Was he a random pick like the serial killers with smarts he had seen on one of his favorite shows, *Joe Kenda: Homicide Hunter.* No motive, no connection and if his guy was thorough enough, no nothing. And if he did target him specifically well, that would push things from just plain old scary to flat out terrifying in no time at all. No time to think of anything else, humanize yourself, isn't that what Kenda says to do? Yes, humanize. Make them realize that you are a living breathing person with people and family and feelings and friends and a name! Yes, you have a name and people will miss you and someone, ANYONE is sure to be looking for you at this very moment! Above all else, not an object to simply be discarded. No, certainly nothing like that.

"Sir, I am just a gym teacher from who gives a shit Florida. My name is James. My friends and family call me Jim Junior." he looked down at his feet and conceded, "unfortunate to be called Jim Junior and be a gym teacher. What...what is your name?" He asked in his most head tiltingly genuine human response that he could muster. "I...I have a family...do you...do you have a family?"

The man smirked for the briefest of moments and let go of the throttle and powered off the engine. The boat immediately slowed puttering down to a near standstill in seconds. The face of the man driving the boat had evil thoughts scattered amongst it but then it started to give for the very first time in this long and miserable ride.

It was not a look of wry and twisted humor but a look of sympathy almost? He couldn't quite tell or read this man at all. The boat swayed up and down on the relatively low tide and began to drift starboard a bit now because no one was technically or metaphorically, at the wheel anymore.

Jim Junior tensed as the man approached him slow and sure, making certain as to not capsize the relatively small craft. The hardened looking man managed to look soft for a moment, as he knelt before good old Jim Junior and closed their distance ever so steadily until they were face level. Eye to eye. The man moved his hand slowly up to James Everett Junior's cheek. The gym teacher flinched, but the man's hand held steady still, continuing on until the backside of his hand caressed the side of his cold wet teary cheek. He felt like screaming in protest but decided against the notion in favor of seeing just exactly where this bizarre and uncomfortable moment was going. The man's hand continued slowly passed his cheek and downward to his neck. Jim Junior's freak the fuck out O-meter was shifting into overdrive as the hand passed from collarbone to chest, and it showed. It was written over every goddam inch of his, oh so readable, face. He started squirming slowly, even now, trying not to offend. "Whoa...whaa...what are you doing?" he stuttered as the man's hand neared lap level. The man raised his other hand quickly at first but got slower as he brought it closer, sending Jim Junior's face back to it's original position to avoid it.

He folded all of his fingers into his hand except the pointer and placed the single forefinger over his lips as if to say "shhhhhhhh..." and then resumed his downward journey south whilst maintaining the sweetest, sickest grin to ever befall a human face at once before. His mouth seemed to widen the closer his hand got to James Junior's sensitives. He reached JJ's upper thigh and just as his captive audience was about to mount a full-fledged second attempt at a protest. The man clutched the teacher's testicles in their entirety, in what had to have been the world's largest fucking hand, he sent his captive into a backwards reeling motion that left him propped up against the bench of the boat and nowhere else to go, but to scream in agony.

While Jim screamed, the ever so cruel man that was causing him this unique pain, smiled as he twisted and crushed his balls into oblivion. Jim had enough time to think, "me and my big fucking mouth" and once again, he passed into unconsciousness.

The dark man, now very pleased and still smiling, let his grip loose and slowly stood back up, walked over to his makeshift chair, restarted the engine and continued on the path he had been on before he was so rudely interrupted.

The man in the bottom of the boat slept uneasy again, dreaming dreams that went from bad to worse. He dreamed all the way back to his age of eight. An undertow had grabbed at him maliciously, pulling him down and down and down. What was he to do? What could he have done? The ocean moved mountains.

It had happened so fast. Seven seconds had passed from the time of realization that there was a problem, to actually being pulled beneath the surface. Time passed by slowly, oh so slowly, in a salt water washing machine. After about ten seconds of that, you finally realize… your time is up.
Even at age eight, you go, "Uh-oh."
You are out of strength, out of air. You shake, convulse and contort until almost instantly, you go mad and pull in that horrible salt choked mass of pain and nastiness. So bad, that if you were to swallow it, it would feel life ending or altering at best.
However, to pull it into your lungs in the stead of air? That my friend is agony, and the man in the bottom of the boat, waiting unconscious like, for a good old fashioned drowning, was aged thirty-seven. The boy already drowning in his mind, aged eight.

There he was, having a grand day at the beach for his summertime birthday and then he was at his last oxygenated second before the inevitable. That stinking knowledge of what was to come. And then all of a sudden and without warning, he was free of it. He had risen up and out with ease in a slow, dreamlike state, then that rush of air. You just can't get it in and then out again fast enough.

Eventually, after being dragged onto the beach and regaining his full wits, he would regale everyone and anyone who would listen, about his tale of horror and woe, that he would truly never quite get over. A story of the near breathing of ocean and that split second moment in time. A moment that seemed to branch off into an eternity in his mind, where he was sure he was about to die. He would still go to the beach, but when he did, he wore jeans. He would roll up the cuffs of those pants like he was Huck Finn or some body. But what he would not do, under ANY circumstance, was ever willingly; get all the way in the water again.

CHAPTER FIVE:

THE LONG WALK:

THREE WEEKS EARLIER

A boy named Brian stepped out into the school hallway where there didn't seem to be a soul. This seamed to scare him even more than he was already. He was only fourteen but didn't look a day over eleven. He was a medium height for his age at best and a generally unassuming boy. He was a good student, and in his mind, a good student was ever only alone in a hallway to or from the bathroom.

Not doing either of those things, he was completely unsure of his surroundings. He was late leaving his last class, which meant he was late getting to his next class. He was never late.

He did not feel good one bit. He wanted to go home, but how could he just up and leave? Some of the other kids in this school talked about ditching school and some of those even actually did it, but he was not one of them. Uh-uh. He felt queasy and the world seemed tilted and bent to him. He had heard the term surreal used before and this was the first time he felt he understood it's meaning. Walking uneasily down the schools longest corridor it seemed to him like one of those funhouses where the room turns. The walls were pearly gate white and the carpet a deep dark brown. All of the classroom doors were a lush and vibrant red.

He walked along the wall, nearly scraping his shoulder the whole way down. He seemed to be floating in his own mind as if slowly cruising down the hall passed the doors on what could only be described as one of those airport conveyer belts. The ones that moved the people that could not bring themselves to walk the airport from beginning to end. Each red door had a rectangular window whose vertical sides were long and offered glimpses into the room in it's entirety. If you crammed your face in it, you looked like Nicholson with his face protruding through the bathroom door savagely announcing, "HEEEEEEERE'S JOHNNY!" in *The Shining*, one of his favorite movies.

Every time he passed one of those red windowed doors he was sure the entire class was looking at him. He would stare in eerie anticipation of what was to come, fixated on the soon to be rectangle window from hell. It was as if each room knew, that at that precise moment, KNEW he was coming by.

The hallway was only about a hundred or so yards long, but it may as well have been a mile. He arrived at his classroom on auto pilot. Have you ever driven a good long distance with starts and stops, left turns and rights and everything in between? And when you finally arrive at your destination you realized you had been thinking of a billion other things and had no good goddamn earthly idea how in the hell you actually got there? This was that moment for him.

His hair was damp and palms sweaty. He wiped them on his jeans to dry them and the moment the hands left denim they became instantly sweaty again. He reached for the doorknob. It felt steely cold in his grip and steamy hot in the next moment, as he turned it in an attempt to open the door. At that very second, the sound of air being sucked into a pressure sealed room caused every student and the teacher to cease whatever that it was they were doing, the very moment prior. As every student's head turned his way for real, for the first time since his long journey from class to class began, he wanted to climb inside himself and never come back out. In reality it was much simpler than that. In reality, they all looked at him the way they would have all looked at anybody. Anyone breaking the pressure barrier of this class, which was over sixteen minutes into itself.

His teacher, Mister Harless, or Mister H as the hipper kids called him, taught Spanish Language sessions one through four at that high school for seventeen years. He was writing on the chalkboard with his back to the door. At a glance, one could read certain words scrawled in Spanish from left to right. "Por favor" was one; "ayudame and Lo Siento" were among others, so on and so on. He turned his head while continuing to write the word "solamente". The teacher had a look of surprise on his face, as did most everyone else. "Hola! Senor Anderson!"
The boy stood, stupidly silent.
The teacher tried again. "Senor Anderson?"
The word stumbled out lifelessly.
"Hola."
"Hola. Donde has estado, Senior Anderson?" then to the class, "where, have you been?"
The boy just stared. Mildly annoyed at the lateness and unusual lack of response but not wanting to devote any more school time to the matter he spoke English directly to the student, which in Mr. Harless' class was truly, "no bueno."
"Mr. Anderson, sit down." The boy looked slowly around the room at the myriad of faces waiting for a move, an answer, anything. He cut this long miserable moment short with a quick apology.

"I'm sorry Mr. Harless, it won't happen again" he spoke softly and sat down at his desk as all heads returned to the front of the class and Mr. H continued writing.

Mr. Anderson sat thru the teacher's lesson droning on in the background, just out of reach to be fully heard. "El Mariachi, something or other" he heard and pulled from the haze around him. He was beyond all of that now. He took out his notebook and began writing in it the way the rest of the class had been doing, before his arrival. He wrote on and on, barely looking anywhere but down for the next twenty-five or so minutes until the bell rang signifying the end of class. He slid his notebook and pen from his desk directly to his bag and was out the door fast, amongst the first to leave.

The hallways were teaming with students breaking free of their last class of the day. Streams spilling into the tributaries, all searching for the ocean. The sea refused no river.as they poured out of the front doors heading for their cars. Heading for home, walking in all sorts of directions. Mr. Anderson hurriedly walked in an entirely different direction altogether.

The school's south end of the property bordered a patch of woods and some hilly hills, that depending where you lived in town could be only a ten minute walk. But if you tried to drive it by roads and side streets, it would take you nearly a half an hour. Unfortunately, it was a dangerous path filled with darkness and some falls and with only a smattering of daylight. There was just enough light to pierce the tree line and hit the ground. There was an assortment of possible Florida wildlife to consider as well. Not too long ago a twelve foot long gator managed to get itself within 15 feet of the main entrance before anyone had even realized he was there. So yeah, there was about a half mile of tall fence bordering the parking lot and the forest like hilly hills. He made straight for it, not running but looking like he was always on the verge. Some kids had gone in there a few times to drink and fool around and managed to cut the chain link in the far corner. It was small enough to go unnoticed by most adults. Certainly large enough for a fourteen year old going on eleven. He would go there sometimes to be alone and now, he had to be.

He had gotten to the far corner and reached down and grabbed the bottom corner of the cut loose chain link fence He lifted it up and crouched just enough to clear it. He had made his way down the little dirt ramp that he would shuffle down to avoid the small but steep fall to the little trees at the bottom. He came skidding to a stop, as all of the kids that had passed through here did. Of all the times that all of the kids did this same act, this is the first time they weren't enjoying it. He reached out and grabbed one of the skinny trees. They were the kind that with enough effort could be bent or broken from the ground and used as an oversize and inefficient, walking stick.

He gripped his brand new walking stick super tight with his right hand and lost his lunch. All of it. A bad slice of high school cafeteria pizza, fries and a twelve-ounce apple juice. His stomach squelched and twisted and turned, until there was no muscles left to hold it into position anymore and his body gave. He stood there, choking one moment and hyperventilating the next. His chest rising and falling like a sleeping bears would. His chest was heaving and burned from sheer exhaustion, mixed with some vomit he had managed to breath back into his lungs. He slowed for a moment and then he threw up again. This time it was just bile and the third was as dry as a bone. Nothing at all.

His hyperventilation slowed and he began to feel the hurting pain hidden until now, in his ribs specifically and his whole body in general His head pounded from the strain of the heaving type of puking he was doing and it seemed as if his legs wanted out of this bullshit situation too, but they behaved as if they might make it. His right hand was gripping the skinny tree so tightly; it was making his knuckles a jaundiced, whitish yellow. His left hand was propped up on his left knee doing it's best to keep the rest of him from collapsing to the ground. At this point, he was still standing due to the sheer physics of the way he was positioned or merely by the grace of God. His mind no longer just reacting, but at the beginning stages of thinking again. He started to slowly loosen his grip on the poor, now bent skinny tree and color began to slowly return to his fingers and palm. His breathing became less panicked with time, slowing, slowing. He stopped breathing all together for a second as if he had seen someone nearby. Then released his air to the world in a hysterical smattering guffaw that almost instantly turned to crying himself blind and drooling, all in the span of about three seconds. It was a silent, painful cry. It was the kind of cry a small child has when they are so upset, so besides themselves, that they cannot seem to remember how to breathe.

He dropped to his knees, grasping the loose dirt, grass and rocks in his palm and between his fingers. He caught a small ragged stone in the pile held with his right hand and was squeezing so hard that he drove the sharpest edge of the rock through the meat of his palm beneath his thumb. Blood flowed freely. He did not notice.

His breathing began to slow again. He nodded his head up and down as if a final agreement had been struck with someone standing there with him. His face suggested that whatever deal had been conjured, it sounded like the right answer had been found. He pushed his hands up from the ground sending his top half vertical again and rocked him back until he was just on his knees. He wiped his face with his shirt. He barely got anything, and what he did get he simply managed to smear to a different location or actually add more dirt. He reached back up to the surrounding skinny trees and used them to help himself up. Once there, he leaned back an inch and reached for his bag. It had a little barf on it. It had slid down his shoulder to his arm when the ralphing had started. Normally that would be a big deal, but he hadn't the will to deal with something as trivial as his own second helping of lunch. The boy started to walk and dragged his bag almost lifelessly at his side. He began walking up the hillside, heading towards sunset at the crest, which would be here mere hours from now.

He slogged along for what felt like forever but in fact was only about ten minutes.

When he finally reached the top he let his bag fall all the way to the ground and just stared silently into the sky. The sun sat huge in it. It seemed *SO* big to him. I mean, yes, the sun is big, but this was ridiculous. He had imagined himself back in science class, weeks earlier, when his science teacher Mr. Nguyen, tried to give the class perspective when considering the size of the sun. He had told them that the sun was in fact, so large, that it could fit one point three million earths inside of it. He thought Mr. Nguyen was being a tad exaggerative but he looked it up when he got home and was stunned to find it was right. ONE POINT THREE BILLION.
Perspective?

He could barely get a grip on the nature of the earth and all of what it represented from sea to shining sea. One point three...BILLION.

What about the solar system? What about the galaxy? And what about the universe, and tomorrow? He couldn't even get his head around tomorrow.

The wind picked up. He was all alone and the sun was getting lower and lower in the sky. He heard creaking tree limbs and snapping twigs somewhere in the not too far off distance. It occurred to him that those sounds could be being made, by somebody near. Someone he had not noticed? He had thought he was alone, but just how long had he been sitting here anyway? Had he been making any real noise? He knew he wasn't being exactly what the librarians would call quiet, per say, but that was sometime ago now and far away from here. Could anyone have really heard him at all? He felt like he was being watched. It was the same feeling he got when he was gliding passed the classroom doors. Only this time the classrooms were on the conveyor belt, not him. He didn't think he had to worry, but since he didn't like the thought and was getting more uncomfortable by the minute, he decided to get up and go anyway.

He stood straight and breathed in the hilltop air deeply; taking in the pre night sky in all of its splendor. He exhaled and started down the other side of the hill making to the bottom just one hour before sunset. As he cleared the woods he slowed and took another deep breath all the way to the very back of his lungs, as far back as they would allow, then slowly and deliberately sighing it back out again. He looked around at the valley and a calm came over him. He kicked a rock that was laying at his right foot it flew about ten feet and then bounce rolled a few steps. And there it stayed, more or less, for the next twenty-two years.

Young Mister Anderson drifted towards the street at a more normal pace, if not a bit slower. It was when you were walking home from school with a bad report card kind of walk. He finally reached his neighborhood and headed down his block until he came upon his house and headed straight for the side of it. He peeked around the driveway slow. A white van was parked in the back corner of the driveway. Mom was home and she would almost certainly be wondering where he had been, while herself being knee deep in making dinner. He would have to be quiet, as she was most certainly going to have questions if she saw how filthy he had gotten. He was a young boy and young boys tended to get dirty, but he was not the play in the dirt with the bugs, kind of kid. He never was and he never would be.

He crept up to the side of the house to where the faucet was and he turned the handle slowly, allowing water to come out a bit heavier than a trickle and was sure to not turn so far as to let it go full geyser. He struck that perfect balance and with a semi rusty copper squeak, he was able to wash his hands and face and dust his clothes off. The clothes weren't exactly spotless, but it was the best it was going to get with wet hands whacking off dried mud could. He stood up straight again and caught his reflection in one of the windows along the sidewall of the house. He tussled his hair for a moment and tried on a casual smile. It seemed to fit okay. He could see the cracks in the armor, but if you were none the wiser you may gloss over such subtleties.

He breathed in slow again, one long deep breath, to collect himself for one final moment. As he did, he noticed the air again. It had smelled different here than it had the last place he had just done this. It smelled of oil in his driveway. Oil and pavement. The drive had been redone almost two years ago, but the smell remained. If he had been standing a few more feet towards the back of the driveway, he would also be able to smell the old rotting paint on the garage. That was long overdue as well and it reminded him of the smell of the funeral parlor he had recently attended twice before. His father's mother and father had died not even six months apart from each other. They had been married for sixty three years and passed on, one right after the other. He had heard that happens sometimes. When you have a couple that was so in love and spent nearly every waking moment with each other during their tenure, that they couldn't sustain life without the other.

It was a sour and sad smell. Funny what smells can do when it comes to placing us directly into a time and place, isn't it?

He was startled, as the sprinklers kicked on like a team of angry rattlesnakes, the way they had at the stroke of sunset ever since he moved here at the ripe old age of three.

Across the street, the unmistakable sound of the abominable prize Rottweiler, Jeter. An all Pitch Jet Black Roti if you've ever seen one. If you don't have a frame of reference, imagine the expression that the two small, brown patches of fur above the Rottweiler's eyes that substitute for eyebrows, can convey or allow. Especially, the look of levity or happiness. Now, take that all away. An expressionless, emotionless eternal void of a killing machine. Its eyes were all filled with black, it had seemed. He could never, nor would he ever if he could help it, get close enough to see otherwise. Those eyes were so dark in fact; they seemed to blend with its pitch dark fur as well. If you were enough of a good distance away, it would almost seem as if it had no eyes at all.

Satan dog with a black wall where it's eyes should be and yellow teeth stained from the stream of small animals and neighborhood children it had devoured in his mind. It reminded him of Quint's speech in Jaws. About, "Lifeless eyes. A doll's eyes…"

Bone chilling.

He gathered himself together; still inspecting the new rent a smile and then turned and headed towards the back entrance to the house, which lead him directly into the kitchen and his mother.

She was moving busily from stove to refrigerator, to counter top and back again, making one of her signature dishes and one of his personal favorites. Chicken Fettuccini Alfredo.

"Hey Honey. How was school?"

"Fine." he answered plainly.

"Just fine? That doesn't sound like my usual school loving lad." she quickly moved on. "Home a little later than normal, all okay?"

She paused for a moment to listen to his reaction, still slowly stirring her wares.

"Yeah, I stopped at Freddie's on the way."

Freddie's was on old school video arcade that still managed to have a whole bunch of stand alone video consoles from the early eighties and nineties like Asteroids and Frogger as well as the like of Mortal Kombat and Time Crisis.

"Ahh, game day. I see." she said.

His mother seemed to understand the games thing. She had him at the ripe old age of twenty, which is more a fringe uneducated thing nowadays and was more the standard the thirty years to God knows when centuries and millennia prior. So she could relate to him in such fashions. It wasn't too long ago she had been playing video games herself. The world of entertainment had been their biggest connection. Especially the movies and Stephen King books, their favorite of course being *The Shining*, the best of both worlds' Stephen King and cinema had to offer at once. They had read once that Stephen King himself was not quite too fond of the Kubrick version. There was a huge war waged with the fans of both, but mother and son loved both separately and with great intensity. Mom had once argued that the movie versions of Stephen King adaptations were always labeled on the posters and in the credits as *Stephen King's* this or *Stephen King's* that, but for the 1980 version of *The Shining*, it said *Stanley Kubrick's The Shining*. For a reason, at that "Could you imagine the cinematic shit that would have befallen the topiary animals sequence in 1980?" she would say. "That awful Mick Garris televised version decades later, will still be happy to demonstrate, for example."

Boy, did he love Mom.

She had noticed a touch of melancholy on him, but nothing she felt was too out of the ordinary for a fourteen year old boy. These were the odd and awkward years of zits and hormones and girls and voice changing. And girls, did I mention girls?

Awkward, but nothing she would have considered Abby-normal, a word from another of their favorite movies, a comedy that got play in their home at least twice a year.

They spoke briefly about dinner and after homework, if would he like to come back down stairs to hang out with his rusty crusty ole mom and maybe watch something together? Throughout this conversation, neither of them makes much of any eye contact with the other. Not because she wasn't a good attentive mother or in serious maternal love with her boy in every way. Or that he wasn't wanting of her attention, because he was. She was just so all consumed by her current task of dinner preparations, which occurred six nights a week during this very time frame. From this instant, until her remaining thirty-seven years would pass, she would remember every moment of their last meeting and conversation. Every touch, every sound, every look, every silence and every smell. The meal that was at the top of his list of favorites that would sit on the stove uneaten just a short time from then. The one that would never be cooked in her kitchen again. To the soft but firm and long hug he had bestowed on her as he spoke the words to her. The words that would be their final exchange.

"I Love you Mom."

"I love you too Son." she replied, smiling as he held her fast.

She slowed for just a minute, relishing each moment of that hug, letting dinner sit and wait, confusedly then and much, much differently now.

Those words echoed for eternity within the walls of her mind. For a long time to come she would blame herself for not being less busy, for not being more attentive, for not taking one extra second to smell the roses.

For all of it.

He released her and she kissed his forehead as he walked towards the stairwell to his room. He put his cell phone in his pants pocket and as she turned her back to resume her dinnerly duties, he cruised by the back kitchen counter and swiftly removed her cell phone and slid it into his other pants pocket, unnoticed. He made his way from the kitchen and started up the long walk of stairs to his bedroom, his last such climb, and made one last call.

"I love you Mom", he thought.

"Forever. "

CHAPTER SIX:

THE BIG BAD WOLF: PART ONE

Jim Junior, then gym teacher, once again, out cold. There he lay, in the bottom of a glorified metal dingy with a small but sturdy outboard engine, no less. Suddenly and without signal or sign, he snapped too. He jerked backwards, hair wet from the cold water that had been collecting slowly in the bottom of their boat.

They had picked up speed again. His captor looked down at him and semi smiled. Things seemed to be getting funnier and funnier to the man behind the wheel and it was not making James Junior feel the least bit better about it or his progress. His wrists and ankles still bound and tied, hurting more and more, but even still was nothing that compared to the steady heaving and throbbing nightmare that were his balls. At first, he had forgotten precisely how they came to feel that way, but yes. Yes, it was all coming back to him now.

This fucking weirdo nearly kissed me, he thought to himself.

It was as if the man behind the wheel had heard this thought or at the very least, read it right off of the bound man's face. Because at the very same moment he had thought it, another sick sweet smile, not unlike the one he got during the oddball caressing of his face, crept up on the mean looking man's mug. The look made him shudder. He felt violated by the man's last actions towards him and even more so thinking there was even the slightest possibility that he could see into his mind.

He was afraid to speak out to the man again, but he was even more terrified at the prospect of drowning. Well, more than the agony that may accompany too many more annoying questions or statements anyway. He felt like he had tried everything. Talking, reasoning, begging, but this guy just wouldn't budge. He felt like he was on the verge of going mad with indignation. He had always felt in control of everything. Most of all, the events that occurred in his life, with the exception of his near death drowning incident as a young boy. I think that was why he always sought to be in control of everyone and everything. It was the opposite of what he had felt that day on the beach before the outside ocean was about to invade the interior of his lungs. He needed his sense of control and right now, he had none. He was at the whim of this madman. As far as Jim Junior was concerned, he didn't have a pot to piss in or said window, to throw it out. All he had was his throbbing testicles and a massive goddamn headache. He as a human being in general, fucking ached.

How? …How, How, HOW?! How, the FUCK did this happen to

him?

His anger boiled just below the surface the way lava would on an angry and active volcano. It simmered and stewed and boiled and grew. The driver of the boat could see it was all about to happen and he held a bemused look upon his face that seemed to turn into a coy smile laced with satisfaction. The frustrated man who lay bound and tied erupted into an animal like roar as he screamed, "WHO THE FUCK ARE YOU??!!" He seemed to yell so hard and so intense that veins rippled through his neck and drool spilled from his lower jaw as his body lost all strength and muscle. Jim Flannigan slumped over on his side; he shook in raw fear and fury.

CHAPTER SEVEN:

THE BIG BAD WOLF: PART TWO

Almost four weeks before the boat ride, the rugged, scruff looking man behind the wheel of the boat was crouched down against the outside wall of someone's empty garage. He was trying very hard to not move a muscle or make a sound. Even though it was still technically daylight (though just before sunset), he was dressed all in black with black gloves and a black cap. The spot in which he lay hidden in was under some trees and shadows. It helped blend him in with them nicely. He peered gently around the corner of the garage and saw a car approaching off in the distance, finally, heading his way. Could this be the one he was waiting for all this time? He surmised it could be and that old surge of adrenaline resurfaced, giving him the sharp focus he needed for such tasks.

He could feel that anxious cold sweat coming on that occurred frequently when he found himself performing duties like this. It was everything. It was a high and he loved it. Needed it even. HE wouldn't call it that, but that is exactly what it was.

The car got closer and closer with every passing moment and with every passing moment, he begun to realize, it was not slowing down. His muscles, once tense and ready and prepared to wreak havoc, loosened for the time being and began waiting the good wait again. The car sped on by, unyielding in its travels as it was headed way out of town. Headed north to Atlanta, Georgia, in fact, to a birthday party the day after next. Then, silence again. This type of activity that he seemed destined to perform over and over came with a lot of silence. A lot of silence and a lot of waiting, a known risk in this line of work. One had to have patience and lots of it. You had to have the will to wait it out longer than the other guy, and HE did. His philosophy was if this asshole thinks he can hold his breath for two minutes, you have to be willing and able to hold yours for four. You had better be able to morph yourself into a goddam humpback whale. Hold your breath like it mattered, because it did. Sometimes if you couldn't, if you broke the surface and took that massive breath seeming to lie just out of reach, dying to break it's way back into your oxygen-starved lungs too soon? Sometimes, a harpoon would be lying in wait of you, instead of you for it.

So he just sat there and he waited. Cool. Calm. Thirty seven more minutes had gone by, but after the previous five and a half hours, what was another thirty seven? His legs were a tad stiff but considering how long he had spent crouched down with them it could and should have been, a hell of a lot worse. He wanted to get his hands on this one bad. A long time he had watched and waited and he would have his way. He had hovered over and watched and waited like this a dozen or more times over the years, but few he had wanted more than this. This was for him and him alone. Just then, as hope seemed to abscond and had just as quickly returned. A car approached, headlights on. Even during the day, strong headlights could obscure the front end design of the vehicle, causing year make model and color difficult to discern. The size and shape seemed right and it was traveling slow enough to raise his suspicions. Then the slow car began to slow down even more.

"This is it" he thought.

The driver was even kind enough to put their blinker on well in advance of the turn, alerting him fully to their intentions with this here driveway he had camped out in. The driveway was one of those half circle driveways that entered and exited the road from two different locations. He had hoped dearly that they would turn into the first of the two entrances and not its second. If they didn't and entered from the second turn, then the car would be facing him and not away. The way he had needed them to go and gambled on. There would go his element of surprise.

Bye, bye.

But as fortune would have it, the car turned into the first, and suddenly, from his position he was able to see for the first time, that the driver was not alone.

"Mother Fucker" he thought. "Of course."

This just got complicated. That means more trouble for him and more trouble, he did not need. He removed the glove from his left hand and held it against the dark brick wall from which he was propped up against and raised two fingers on it as if he were giving the wall the peace sign. He put his glove back on and reached around his back and grabbed hold of the forty-five caliber handgun he had waiting in the back of his pants waistband. He pulled it up before his face and checked the safety catch to off and slid back the rail to make sure he had one in the chamber. He did. He always did. Once he had his weapon ready and steady, he made himself small against the garage to make sure he would not be noticed. He did not sit here is discomfort all this time just to throw the game with seconds to go on the clock. The car began its slow left turn into the center of the driveway shaped like the upside down letter U. A man was behind the wheel and a woman sitting in the back seat as if being chauffeured. The man looked as if he could be in his late twenties or early thirties and the woman appeared to be at least five years or so younger than that.

The scruff man waiting with the weapon behind the garage wall was a large man, but the man behind the wheel seemed even larger so. Still, he was unafraid. He looked at things such as these as a challenge. He loved a challenge. The woman, however, was considerably smaller than both men. The man in black would not go so far as to call the woman in the backseat pretty, but comely perhaps, if that makes any sense. She had a look on her face that he could see arousing a few men with a flash of the right smile and the batting of eyes. The big man emerged from the car first. He shut the drivers side door, straightened his grey hoodie, pulling it down over his waistline and he looked around as the wind pushed the hair back and forth on top of his head.

The man in black was stiff with anticipation as a wolf would be amongst prey that were still as of yet, unaware of its presence. Frozen into position, one paw hovering in the purgatory between the heavens and the earth, waiting for the right moment to spring its deadly trap, as the deer picks it's head up from drinking in the brook. The deer looks around, listening to every sound the forest had to offer, smelling the unstill air in hopes that a breeze would carry the forewarning of the scent of a predator on its way. This action on behalf of the deer being watched only lasted about three or four seconds but may as well have been a lifetime for the man in black. The large man moved to the back door just before his closed behind him and opened it for the woman who lies in wait in the back. She emerged, back to the world and seemed to be trudging something out with her, and she was. With her, out came a small baby carrier.

"Fuck", was the thought that came into his head next. He knew it. The moment he saw her in the car too, he knew things were going to go from bad to worse. He didn't want it to go this way, but sometimes the way it was, is the ONLY way. He quickly weighed his options out, what little options there were, took a deep breath and sighed them all away. Such is life, he thought to himself. So, the big question he posed to no one was "Now? Or by the door? "

In the world of complicated, things were about to go from crap to shit, if they made it into that house.

Now, he decided. "NOW!" He yelled at himself, in his mind as he leapt up from his perch and lunged outward like a greyhound chasing an electric rabbit, loosed after the sound of a thousand blazing bells blasting off at Belmont.

The man, still holding the door open for the woman with the baby seat and she holding on tightly, had started to turn towards him. He had managed to close almost half the distance between the garage and the car, but still had a distance to go with hardly any time left at all before they saw him coming. As she turned into his direction, her eyes had grown from the size of nickels to the size of half dollars. It was with this slight change in denomination, that he realized that she had locked her eyes with his. In the next three heartbeats he would close the distance or all would be lost. For the man in black, who had been at a crux like this time and again, it was played out, each heartbeat, in slow motion.

ONE

In the first heartbeat, the woman's eyes widened and she began to suck in a gust of air to the very back of her lungs, with the ferocity of a person who had been unable to breathe until that very moment. As he thrust himself in their direction, he could tell she was trying to sound the alarm to the man holding open the door for her, but it was all coming out in a panicked gibberish.

"de...bug...gee gee!" was all she was able to get out.

The man to her side, still holding the door, was able to react much quicker once he was able to get the message, but alas, that message arrived too late.

His eyes flashed to her face and even though he only could see a complexly bewildered look on it, he was able to instantly read, "TROUBLE!" and his expression changed too, in lightening quick speed.

TWO

In the second heartbeat, the man in the grey hoodie began to turn towards the man in black and reached towards the back of his pants. The man in black read this movement sharply and raised his gun and aimed at the large young man's chest. The woman seemed to be reaching for something as well, still running full charge, the man in black read that as well and followed suit, unholstering a second, smaller caliber weapon from under his right arm.

THREE

In the third of three heartbeats, the young, but large man swung his arm around front, the woman produced a knife as six or seven unmarked police cars careened around the corner, skidding off of the main road and onto the rainbow shaped driveway. The rugged looking man in black saw his last moment arrive before his larger and younger counterpart managed to have his weapon trained lethally upon his body. The woman looked to the oncoming train of police vehicles heading directly to them and began lowering the knife towards the interior of the baby carrier.

The man in black zeroed on this and wasted no more time. He fired twice and struck twice, hitting the young man in the upper right chest and then immediately after, again in his right shoulder. The man flew back, right out of one shoe and both feet completely off the ground, as he slammed his back against the open rear door of the car, breaking its window and bending the hinge eighty degrees in the wrong direction. The charging police vehicles swarmed atop the central location, officers emerging, guns drawn as she lowers the knife within an inch of the baby's throat.

"DON'T!" was all the man in black could manage. And the moment he realized that she had absolutely zero intention of listening to "DON'T!" he pulled the trigger of the pistol in his right hand twice more.

The bullets struck home both times, one right after the other. First in the upper stomach and then again in her chest, just below her heart. The first shot was enough to ensure the dropping of the knife and the baby carrier and the second had blasted her right back into the backseat from whence she came.

The oversized young man on the ground had begun to reach towards the gun he had dropped just a heartbeat or so ago. The man in black officially arrived on scene, stepping on his wrist just before it could make its mission. He still had his gun trained on the woman in the backseat of the car and the other one on lover boy here. She was bleeding profusely from her stomach, chest and mouth. The other police officers surrounded them, training all weapons on both suspects.

"You got 'em?" the Man in black asked sharply.

"Yeah. We got them LT." several officers responded in unison.

The baby was now screaming from the brief shouting and the

thunderous weapons report and shattering glass all over his soft sweet smelling head, clothes and car seat. The man in black was known to all of his fellow officers and detectives as Detective Lieutenant, "LT" or Bob of the Tampa Florida Police Department. He worked feverishly but ever so gently to remove the buckles and straps holding the baby securely in his seat. He scooped the infant up and cradled it close to his heart, rubbing his back and soothing him the best he could. He had not done this in a long time His phone, in its holster on his hip, buzzed furiously and he reached down and silenced it with a swift and easy motion as he was used to doing in times like these. He took a handkerchief from his pocket. "Give me some water!" he shouted to anyone and everyone. Two officers appeared at his side in seconds, each offering up a fresh bottle of water each. He reached out blindly and snatched the first one to hit his palm, opened it and poured it all over the cloth he had. He wrung it out in his one hand as it went from sopping wet to just damp in a moments time, and he began wiping the smatterings of blood from the baby boy's face.

Paramedics were already on scene and were attending to the two downed suspects, growing ever colder from the dramatic blood loss caused from wounds such as theirs. The man on the ground was writhing and cursing. No doubt due to his piss and vinegar disposition, he seemed like he may actually be just fine after a nice little hospital stay, some minor surgery and some painkillers given at minimum intervals. Unfortunately for this joker, the good docs at the local hospital had never been sympathetic in the narcotics department when it came to assholes endangering children.

The detective had a slightly different opinion of the young woman's fate as she choked and gagged and spat blood violently, all over the backseat. Screaming and crying at the knowledge and fear that accompanied the realization that you were dying and soon.

He turned his head to the left when he heard someone say "lieutenant". He thought he might have been imagining it as there was another lieutenant on site and the cry seemed to be coming from far away. But no, there was a uniformed medic waiting in his face as he turned.

"Lieutenant?" the man asked again.

LT looked back at the baby, starting to settle down in his arms and seeming to find comfort in gazing in the Lieutenant's eyes and then back to the medic before him.

"I'll take him from here sir." He said soft and matter of factly.

The man looked down briefly in a nod to the baby and quickly returning his gaze to the lead Detective, quietly hinting that he meant to take the baby. It seemed like his words were running aground here. Bob looked back down, the baby holding his forefinger in a tight baby grip. It brought a smile to the corners of his mouth and the baby seemed to return it, in kind. He slowly brought the child's hand to his mouth and kissed it ever so gently. It was unlike him to show such a display. Very unlike him, but he remained unconscious about it. He wasn't an emotionless man by any means. It was just that he had seen so much horror in his life. His career on the force of some twenty years. His work. He would tell his wife in a random comment produced from a recliner, some time ago. It wasn't a conversation or even an exchange. He was sitting there drinking whiskey on ice, his favorite painkiller, and just blurted it.

"I've lost a piece of my humanity, my darling dear. A big fucking piece."

So now, in this late stage of a long and storied career, it took quite a bit for him to react to something with emotion on a scene. There was a time where he would marvel at a sunset or a work of art, Dali in particular, or waved at a group of small children getting off a school bus. But now, for the most part, he was reserved and more than a bit shy about emotional outbursts like this one. Even though it was something as small and simple, as brushing a baby's hair back to comfort him. To whisper in his ear that everything was going to be okay. For him, the gesture was grand. His phone buzzed again signaling a message had been left after the constant buzzing from just moments ago.

He looked up at the paramedic still staring at him and he gently lifted the baby in his direction, the medic getting underneath, received him. He carted the baby off to the ambulance quickly. "Okay, lets move!" the medic barked to the driver.

The back doors slammed as they settled the child in and drove off to have a good once over, on the seemingly fine, baby boy. The Detective was about to check his blinking phone when another man in a suit approached.

"Hey Bob. You got a second? You have to take a look at something we found over here."

Bob collected himself for a moment. The other Detective turned and began to walk away the moment he asked his question, assuming the rhetoric in said question was implied. Responding in similar fashion, the Lieutenant spoke out, "yeah." to absolutely no one at all and followed, just a handful of steps behind his colleague back to the crime scene's ground zero. The car.

He approached the vehicle from the far side, where the shooting had just, minutes earlier, taken place. There were three paramedics left on the scene, in various stages of repair as well as clean up. Two of them worked the still clinging to life male suspect and the third was working through those final, futile last ditch attempts at saving the woman's life, as was protocol. Attempting to salvage the unsalvageable.

She had ceased choking three minutes earlier and her shallow breathing downgraded to no breathing at all, in a hurry. Her last blood filled gargle got caught in her throat, as her lungs were simply too weak to give the necessary thrust to keep themselves going and the choking, to keep on choking. No air in and no more out, it all just stopped, as we all one day, do.

Her bowels had released during the moment when the two bullets had made impact with her chest and stomach and she had already smelled bad. Her eyes were fixed on the scratched felt ceiling with the cracked dome light that had caught a long dead, decent sized mosquito in it. The other bystanders were all busy doing their own various tasks, focused on different things. But the soul, still trapped in her recently dead body, wasn't. It was trapped here for another few minutes of brain activity. Gawking awkwardly at shitty ceiling scratches and nasty insects and cigarette burns in a crappy old model Ford Fuck You Mobile, for Eternity.

Hell, on earth.

The man was fairing better, more or less. The gunshot wounds and the subsequent blood loss had managed to drain him of enough vital fluids as to keep him relatively docile and without much fight as the paramedics worked to patch him up.

"Sir? We have to move him." The chubbiest of the three said to him without much urgency.

"Do it." Was the Detective's dry response. He turned to the other detective in the car's front seat. "What you got Joe?"

"Bag of money." He stated matter of fact.

"Nice. How much?"

"Uhhhh", he hemmed. "Dunno. Looks like hundreds..." he paused making his hemming sound again, literally wagging his head from side to side three or four times, humming as he decided on the most accurate estimate based on what he was seeing before him. "Ten thousand dollar bundles. I dunno, seventy, maybe eighty thousand. Maybe. I haven't touched the bag yet, so..." he trailed off.

"Okay." Bob responded thoughtfully as the wheels turned in his mind.

"Hey," he continued, "you remember that whodunit robbery over in Ybor a couple of months ago?"

"Yeah." The other Detective scoffed. "You think?"

"Maybe." He said his mind on other things. "Find out how much was the original reported amount missing. It may not line up exactly, it was a nightclub after all" he spoke raising an eyebrow.

He reached down for his phone and with it in hand motioned to the bag of dough in the front seat.

"But before you do any of that, get on some gloves and count that and let me know exactly what we are dealing with here."

"You got it LT." Joe said in agreement and nodding in respect. He lifted his phone and swiped his screen to find the missed call and voicemail left only minutes earlier. He tapped voicemail with his thumb and held the phone to his head. He stood there motionless as he listened. His face was in a slight crunch as he strained to listen and the put his forefinger in his other ear to assist. His face started to unwrinkle and slouch and then seemed to drop altogether. Still holding the phone up to his head he began walking, slow at first and building momentum as he went further and further along the driveway. After his fifth or sixth step he had moved from a fast walk to a run, heading straight for the still running police cars at the end of the drive. He reached the first patrol car he could find and started to climb in, throwing his phone to the passenger seat until he had control of the car.

He slammed the door closed behind him and the owner of that vehicle turned around when he heard it's door close.

"Sir?" was all he could manage in a curious puzzled voice.

"Sorry, I need you car." He said plainly as he cranked the engine on and threw her into drive. He looked away and slammed his foot down on the gas, where it would remain firmly for the next twenty or so minutes. He sped away, tires screeching, catching the attention of the remaining officers and Detective on scene.

The detective, looking puzzled, walked over to the officer standing where the speeding patrol car, up until recently, had just been.

"Officer Ramos! What just happened there?" he nodded in the direction of the fleeing car. "Where did he go?"

"I dunno sir. He just said he that he was taking the car."

"Then what?" he asked, arms extended out from his side in frustration.

The officer looked confused and answered accordingly.

"Then, he uh…he did. Sir."

The Detective rolled his eyes.

"Christ! You and You." He ordered, pointing at two of the officers. "Go after him."

The two cops climbed in their cruiser and high tailed it out of there. The Lieutenant had gotten a few minutes head start and he was driving like a bat out of hell, so they had their work cut out for them.

He sped down the road with his phone back on his ear.

"COME ON!" he yelled into the receiver. "FUCKING ANSWER!" he demanded. But there was no answer.

Nor would there ever be.

CHAPTER EIGHT:

WOE, IS ME

The man powering the boat let go of the handle and the engine puttered out, slowing the boat with it. The night sky seemed clear and infinite and now with the engine off and the noise from it, gone, all that remained was the sound of the sea. The boat's Captain stood up and made his way over to the man bound foot and ankle.

Jim Junior was still mending from some bad memories during their last encounter and could not help himself when he recoiled in horror at the man's advancement. This made Bob, the scruffy man, smile. He bent down and reached out towards him. Jim Junior screamed out in protest.

"DON'T! Don't you fucking touch me!" he screamed pulling and squirming back as far as the boat would allow.

The scruff looking man knelt before him and hoisted him up on the seat for the first time. Even though Jim was still scared stiff, sore and sick, still bound wrist and ankle, he was also SORT OF comfortable for the first time as well. The man sat back and smiled. It was a satisfactory smile that bordered on transcendence. There were parts of the night sky, at the very edges of the earth, that had begun to brighten from black to a deep purple and ever so slightly.

The gym teacher had begun to fear that this was it. They had stopped. The man seemed creepily calm. There was a distinct shade of euphoria drifting across his gaze that sent waves of nausea upon him. Jimbo was one motion shy of him giving a full upheaval and barfing all over this metal deathtrap. He did not intend to have what happened next, happen.

He did not intend to, yes and he tried to stop himself, but at this stage of the game, there was no stopping something like this, and with that, he started to cry. What was worse was that it wasn't some staged act or some cheap ploy or attempt at sympathy. It was real. He had nothing left and just crumbled inward and what was worse than that, he might have asked himself? He heard something else that he hated even worse than crying in front of another human being. Crying and talking at the same time and it was HE that was doing it. Oh, how he loathed everything about himself, mentally and physically, right now. How his mind and body could come together as one and completely betray him at this very moment was unbelievable. "Bastards" he thought.

"Oh God Sir, please don't. Don't fucking drown me please! I nearly drowned as a boy and ohhh I am begging you please!"

He likened this kind of crying, the equivalent to the "crying with a mouthful of food in a roomful of people" cry which is to say, horrifying.

"PLEASE" he continued and followed that pride swallowing gesture with a good solid thirty seconds of openly sobbing.

The man looked upon him tilting his head just a little. The way you might if you had just laid eyes on a five legged dog or a three headed chicken for the first time. Then, he breaks his silence with a rapturous laughter that at that precise moment, Jim Junior had realized through his long pathetic existence that this was the single most disturbing sound he had ever encountered and truly ever heard. While he was cowering at the sound of the sick and twisted man's laugh and the man, through his thunderous howling, reeled his head backwards and ever so slightly. He became aware for the first time, that there was a small fishing knife on the floor behind and between the laughing man's legs. "If only", he thought. If only he could lunge and knock the man back. If only he could land the man right into the drink, just long enough for him to get that knife and cut his limbs loose. If only then, he could look over the edge of the boat and laugh hysterically into the now stranded man's face. If only then. He would turn on that engine and drift back to shore, cackling the whole way so the man now stuck drowning in the ocean swells could hear it to his last dying breath! If only. He pondered these things and simultaneously pondered others like, "what if I miss? What if I go over instead? With my hands and feet tied?" Oh Jesus, no. No. "How could he?" He wondered to himself. He didn't have the god damnedest idea. This sent his sobbing into a complete and out of nowhere rage.

"WHAT? WHAT? WHAAAAT?!" This last what seemed to stretch on into forever and the sky lightened by yet another small shade of purple.

"Why are you doing this to me you sick FUCK?! FUCK YOU!, FUCK YOU! Oh, please GOD don't let him drown me!" he trailed off out of energy. "Why?" he said screaming towards the sky. For the first time Bob was unsure if this was directed towards him in particular. "Why are you doing this to me?"

The man kneeled down again. He slowly pulled a small, folded piece of paper from his back pocket. Jim stopped crying. He didn't know what was happening, but he started to get this sneaking suspicion that he was about to get his "Why?"

The man unfolded the paper and spread it out, face up in Jim Junior's lap, smoothing it out gently with his hand and patting it into place. Jim Junior looked up into the man's face and the man's face was watching and waiting. They shared a glance and he felt the man's eyes searching his own and in that look he found the total and utter bliss of satisfaction. He may have liked that look the least. Jim Junior once again looked down in his lap and stared at the writing on the paper. His eyes trying to adjust to the light, or lack thereof as well as adjusting to the up, down, left, right movements the tide was bringing. His eyes settled on sentences and then words. He found himself skimming, lips moving as he skimmed, something he looked down on others for doing. He had skimmed until about midway through what seemed to be a letter and amidst all of the sloppy hand written words, his eyes locked instantly on two. It was his first name, and his last.

There they were, parked right next to each other. He heard a sucking sound and soon after hearing it and wondering where the hell it was coming from, he realized it was in fact coming again, from him as he lifted his eyes from the paper and then to those of his host's. Those happy and yet sad and deeply haunting eyes were just waiting for him.

"Oh GOD", he thought. "I am FUCKED." He continued thinking. And he was.

CHAPTER NINE:

THE WHOLE SHEBANG

The scruffy largely built Lieutenant Detective's tires screeched in agony as he took another corner way too fast.

"COME ON!" he screamed, commanding the phone to "Fucking answer!". But there was no answer, nor would there ever be.

The phone went straight to voicemail for the second time. He cut the wheel a hard right and took yet another tire squealing turn down Castelrock Drive. He slammed his fist and phone against the steering wheel over and over again in a fit of rage and frustration. He could hear his heart in his ears and feel it in his throat. He was not too far away now, he was getting close. He was hitting about ninety down the long side streets slowing just enough at intersections to not kill any innocent pedestrians or cream another vehicle or other assorted oncoming traffic.

"Not today God. Not today." he said shaking his head in a most disagreeable fashion. He picked up the phone and hit redial once more and as with every prior attempt, this one too went straight to voicemail. The message a gleeful invitation to leave a message with the promise of a call back just as soon as humanly possible, if only you would be kind enough to provide a name number and reason for your call! Don't forget to wait for the beep!

"Come on you! Come on!" he screamed to the universe as the beep to leave said message finally went off.

"I am trying to reach you! This is an emergency, pick up the goddamn phone and call me back immediately! I am on my way, I will be there in just two minutes!"

He tossed the phone to the seat beside him freeing both hands and his full concentration for the task at hand and the road before him. He wanted to throw up but was managing to hold it together. It all came down to the training. For years, over and over and over again. And when it matters most, it is autopilot. He made his final turn and burned the rubber as he did it; tear assing down K Street to number Four hundred sixty nine. He reached the front yard and skid his way to a stop on the, just moments ago, pristine front lawn. He leapt from the car hoping against hope and tore up the front stairs, making all four in one giant running step.

Please God; please don't let me be too late. He prayed as he reached the front door. He asked the question in his mind, for sometimes he found that God would be more likely to answer the questions more often there. But not today. No, not this time, and he felt it.

He plowed through the front door as if it weren't there. Had it been locked? He didn't know but he breached it with such ease he wasn't even sure if it was closed. He headed for the stairwell that went to the second floor landing, but it was towards the back of the house. He yelled out, negotiating the living room furniture as he bulldozed his way through the living room towards the kitchen and the back stairwell.

"BRIAN!"

He screamed, panic all over his voice as it quivered helplessly. This did garner one instant response from within the house, his wife Lila, walking through the final throes of cooking dinner in the kitchen.

"Bob?" she yelled in the back of the house, the question emerged in a higher than normal pitch and was laced with concern.

Her husband, the near twenty year veteran Lieutenant Detective was almost *never* home before seven p.m., let alone five thirty. He had just burst into their home and crashed through the living room with an urgency that was reserved for work and emergency situations only. Yet, here he was. Home early, tearing up the house and screaming their son's name with wild panic gripping each cry. Her husband never panicked and that scared her even further. The truth to her, pushed far beyond her capacity to grasp it.

They, both running in the same direction, slammed into each other at the first floor landing. It was the bridge from the front of the house to the back, the living room to the kitchen. He moved her from his path, gently but firm all at once. She broke in to hysterical fits and tears spilled instantly and everywhere, clouding her vision and preventing her from making it up the stairs without stumbling. She sobbingly called to her son, whom she had last seen ascending these very stairs, towards his room as his father now did at breakneck speeds.

"NO! NOT MY BABY!" she screamed, following about eight or so steps behind her husband, who had just reached the second floor landing and the doorway to their son's bedroom. He tried the handle and it wasn't moving.

Locked.

His son never locked his door, since he had accidentally locked himself in when he was only three. It took his Mom a few minutes to jimmy the door open with a pen tube, but to little baby Brian it felt like a whole hour and he never did it again.

Bob backed up two steps from the door, so that his backside was touching the wall behind him and put *everything* he had into his thrust through the entryway, sending splinters of wood in every which direction and landing him deep inside the room. He stumbled forward and his knee stopped his fall from going any further. He looked up from his position and silence befell this man of action, who had always reacted as he was trained to do in every bad and messed up moment he should ever encounter. He suddenly found himself and for the briefest of moments, completely unable to act, as he saw the image that would stay with him for his remaining sixteen years of heartbreak survived on earth. I say survived, because from this moment on, he truly never lived again. On that sad day, when his body caught up with his soul, he had a heart attack and died in his car while waiting at a stoplight on 54th and Cherry Street. Detective Lieutenant (retired) Robert Anderson, managed in his final moments to have the wherewithal to place the car in park. This had prevented his car from sliding through the very busy intersection ahead and lord knows what else.

There before him and just above, an overturned desk chair, hung his fourteen year old son, Brian David Anderson. Bob leapt to his feet and even though he could clearly see his son's lifeless face and body dangling from his bedroom ceiling fan, the way he had seen countless other people's sons and daughters over the years in varying degrees of this state, he was going to save his son. He was sure of it. He was the lead Detective in the Major Crimes Unit for years and he didn't get to that position without learning a few moves to sidestep death.

Robert Anderson grabbed at his son's lifeless and terribly heavy body. For what he considered a small boy, his son weighed tremendous to him. The Detective lifted just enough to allow some slack from the electrical chord that ran around his neck. It was so tight around him that when it started to give way you could see the chord's design imprinted on his skin. The same chord that until recently, was firmly attached to the family vacuum cleaner. Just then at that very moment, with his boy's lifeless lower half firmly being hoisted and hugged by his father, his mother (still begging God No! the entire journey up the stairs) burst through the shattered hole in the wall where her sweet son's door used to be. Lila saw her stoic, unwavering man's usual looking face, had been switched out by some horrible jokester for this beat red, tear filled one. Holding her boy in mid air, seeing his face swollen and purple, eyes open and bloodshot and bulging. She screamed the loudest, saddest, most painful scream a mother could possibly have to offer. Her husband, hearing that scream, brought him back to her.

"LILA! HELP ME!"

"Oh God, I…uh..I…what do I…?" was all she could manage, holding her hands out palms up, as if to say, "Put the answer here…"

"Grab the chair and undo him quick!" he screamed, struggling to keep his boy in the air and the chord slack.

"NOW!"

She scrambled for the chair, turning it back to its upright position under her son. She wept and cried all the while.

"What did you do, baby? What did you do?" The words floated out from Lila and into the air, but neither of them could have told you who had spoken them.

She trailed off, the waterworks completely uncontrollable now rendering her speech an incomprehensible wet gibberish, as the chord peeled away from her boy's neck.

Their once very alive and sweet son, crumpled over his father's shoulder as he gently lowered him to his bedroom floor, over the vintage Empire Strikes Back rug that Brian had found at a flea market and LOVED. It was the centerpiece of his room for years.

Lila, mother and wife, hovered over him and cried without end as Robert, husband and father, jumped into emergency resuscitation mode and began the useless effort of trying to bring his boy back.

The call he received from his son that precipitated all of this madness dropped just over twenty minutes ago. Even if it had been half that time, it would still be two times, too late. But in this situation, knowing didn't matter. He was going to try. When it came to your child, damn what you know, you are going to try.

He worked his chest and mouth with a rapid regularity, using his only free breaths in between to utter three words, over and over again.

"Come on Brian. Come on Brian."

Pumping his hands up and down on his son's motionless chest and delivering a solid breath into his lungs every few blows.

"Come on Brian."

Lila, loving mother weeping uncontrollably at her boy's side, one arm stretched out. Her hand was on his lifeless arm, her other arm holding herself up, barely avoiding collapse.

Suddenly, after minutes of working and working, Robert just stopped. Hands still on Brian's chest, but now just resting in exhaustion and disbelief. His breathing was heavy and uncontrollable. Lila felt her husband's frantic activity stop and she looked at him, also in disbelief. Their eyes met for the first time since she had entered the room and she saw something on them she couldn't understand. She couldn't understand it because she had never seen it before. It was defeat. She looked longingly into those big eyes that never spoke anything but the truth to her and uttered a question as well as statement. It was all at once, in one weak, wavering word.

"No," she pleaded as she shook her head and her lip quivered without any control at all. Even though it came out as part question, she already knew the answer. She knew it before he stopped. She knew it before he started. Hell, as a mother, she knew it the moment her husband blew through the front door and pushed passed her two hours too early, heading in a frenzy to their baby boy's bedroom. But as unbelievable as it were, there lay Brian, no life on him at all, just a shocked looking expression permanently plastered on his face that seemed to stare off into forever. His body strewn across his Star Wars area rug that lay next to his bed that housed him nights, for the last ten years or so. His Big Boy Bed that he got when he turned five. He was so proud of that bed. No more kiddie car bed, no more safety bar. A BIG BED for a BIG BOY.

Robert slid his left arm under his son's limp head and gently lifted it and pulled his body up onto his. He cradled his boy the way he did when he was just a tiny little man. His little bean. The way he cradled that baby he rescued not just thirty minutes ago.

Oh, how it hurt. It hurt even more when it had dawned on him just how long ago it was, when he had last held his son like this. How long it had been since he had held him in his arms in any capacity. The last time he could truly remember an embrace between them, for more than a passing hug, was when Grandma Louise died.

Brian had taken that hard. He was eleven and it was his first and almost last real dealings with the death of a loved one. All other Grandparents had passed before Brian was making memories. He was truly sensitive to his father's feelings, and since it was his dad's mother who had passed, and his father had as of yet said so much as a single word to anyone about anything all morning, Brian decided to go to him. Brian approached him as he stood besides his mother's coffin.

"I'm sorry Dad."

Was all Brian had said. It was all he could say, knowing his father was never much of a conversationalist. It was all either of them would say during that time at the funeral home. It was all that was needed to be said. Father reached his arm out silently and placed it across son's shoulders as he pulled his boy under the crook of his arm and held him tight. They shared a glance of love and understanding and through two sets of tears managed a small smile between them. Brian managed to feel heaven in that time. His father, not being the outwardly expressive emotional type, gave what Brian recognized as a great and welcome gesture. One that he would cherish and long for again for all of his remaining years. Robert, while always knowing this to some degree or other, thought as we all do. That he had more time than he did, to do something about it.

Laying there, holding and rocking his cradled baby, he brushed back his boy's hair and thought of all the things that they hadn't done and now, would never do.

"I'm sorry Brian." He cried, "Daddy's sorry"

Lila, hearing the resignation in her husband's tone and hearing his voice crack wide open in declaration of love and sorrow, collapsed on her men, both of them. Her face resting on her son's shirt openly sobbing. She had been here on this very spot of him not too long ago and oh, God, how blind and stupid she had felt now. So blind and shocked and stupid, but she had been none of those things. It was all so out of the blue and life was doing what it always had done. It was happening all around and at every moment. The day to dayness of it all, that each and every one of us gets so swept up into.

Robert looked down at his wife, draped over their boy and knew exactly what Lila had been feeling. In many ways, he felt much worse for her and what she must be going through. What did he know about carrying a baby from conception through birth? Not a goddamn thing. Sure he was a willing participant, but to actually feel him grow, for him to be a living breathing part of you. That when he moved you could feel him. And unless you spoke of it out loud, no one else would be the wiser to it ever having happened.

He reached out and touched her on the back of her head. His hand, so large, seemed to engulf it. She always found that large paw comforting whether there were times of trouble or the seas were calm. That hand there always seemed to help. Even today, even now, when nothing was a consolation.

His hand caressed her head a couple of times then slid off the side of her, unable to maintain any sort of strength or consistency, then came to rest on his child's unwavering chest. He felt something there that seemed out of place. He moved his hand away from the place it had come to rest and saw something that was not a part of him or the flannel shirt Brian had been wearing. It was a piece of paper, folded neatly and sticking out of his right breast pocket just enough to be missed in all the pandemonium. He looked at it curiously. He was about to dismiss it, but the nagging part of him that was a Detective Lieutenant, kicked back in and he reached out to it. As reasonable an oversight as this was, given their present situation, he was still unhappy with himself for not catching it right away.

He slowly pulled the paper from the chest pocket and began to unravel it. He had gotten it half open and stopped, now, realizing what this was, that he held in his hands, unprepared to read it.

Lila had heard the crumpling of paper and noticed her husband had grown quite quiet and still, and as upset as she was, found herself also slowing and calming in response to her husband's new disposition. Her eyes looking at her husband's weak and solemn face, which was grave, but had a new certain life infused in it, behind it, some new, different emotion. Then she followed her husband's grave gaze down to the half open paper and immediately understood.

"Oh, God." She nearly gagged, "NO. I can't. Nooo." she trailed off, defeated.

"Lila, I have to." He stated as matter of fact and stared into her eyes with sincerity and a deadly seriousness.

She got hold of herself and she nodded, still choking back tears. "Please, aloud to me. Please Bob. I...I can't, I don't have the strength...to read it myself." Softly weeping again.

Bob looked her over and nodded. He opened the letter to its fullest and began to read it aloud.

CHAPTER TEN:

THE LETTER

DEAR MOM AND DAD,

I'm sorry. I want you to know, it was nothing You or Dad EVER did. I love you both **so** much and am **so sorry** I did this to either of you. I hope you know that, above all else.

My PE teacher, Mr. Flannigan held me after class today and got me alone in the boys' showers. I am so ashamed of what happened. I can't bring myself to write it down. I couldn't face you two with this, because that would mean facing him again and the whole world would soon know and I just couldn't live with that. I have given this a lot of thought and I just can't live with the knowledge that you and him and all of the other students or even myself would hear the details of what happened. You two are the only things that matter to me and I know you would never look at me or treat me different, but everyone else would. It is something I have decided I cannot take. School is hard enough being different, without something like this over me.

I am so SO sorry. I love you both.

I am FOREVER your son and baby boy,

Brian.

CHAPTER ELEVEN:

THELASSOPHOBIA

The scruffy man, the Detective Lieutenant, husband and father, Bob, stared at his prey as he finished gazing at the letter. Jim Junior was quietly replaying the predicament he was in over and over in his head. Throughout his weird and horrifying journey he had taken stock of the amount of trouble he felt he had been in and now realized he would give almost anything to go back to that level of worry, rather than deal with what he had been saddled with now.

"Whoa…wait now…" he started all panicked.

"You listen to me you little fuck! If you even think for one second about denying this or insinuating that my son is mistaken in any way, then I will take that nasty little fishing knife that you have been eyeballing behind me, and gut you with it right here on this boat BEFORE I throw you in, do you understand me?"

He thought, "FUCK" but all that came out was "No…you don't have to do this sir, please. Killing me won't bring Brian back."

The determined father smiled and scoffed.

"That was alliteration, what you did right there…bring Brian back…" He scoffed again and it turned into a full blown laugh this time, "Oh, right. Never mind. You're a gym teacher. You see, alliteration is when…"

A screaming raving Jim Junior cut him off.

"I KNOW WHAT ALLITERATION IS ASSHOLE!" He instantly regretted this.

"Thatta boy." The Detective smiled. "Keep that fire in your belly. It's good to know you can still get it up when you need to."

"Please…"

"Pleeeaase" he said waving him off sarcastically. "Please, please, please, please."

"You guys are all the same," he sniffs. "For twenty years, the craziest sickest, most twisted bastards that I have EVER had the fucking misfortune of encountering, were either full fledged psychopaths that couldn't hide what they were if the took one on one magic lessons with Harry Houdini himself *or* they were slick as shit sociopaths. The wolves hiding amongst the sheep. And whenever kids seem to be involved, it is usually him who is least likely. Some hapless looking nobody shlub like you. But you're not just a nobody, are you Jim? Nope. A priest, a boy scout leader…*a teacher*. People are always so shocked," he said, hands shaking in the air, mocking, "Not me Jim. It is people like you that I look to first. Even if I didn't have a note with a finger pointing to you in it. People that are in a position to... do what you ask? Sure, why not." he continued, "To do whatever it is you sick assholes do, to the young unsuspecting, coming of age and *DEFENSLESS* boys and girls that pass through your revolving doors on a yearly basis." He sat nodding to himself in silence for a moment and then began again.

"That was quite a little racket you most likely had going for yourself there, didn't you?" he didn't see Jim Junior make a move to retort but figured he would stop that anyway by continuing straight on after the question was posed, "and we both know, you did." The scruff and scary Detective stood and looked down upon him, bound and pathetic, the way he wanted him. Then he continued:
"After Brian died, I did some checking on you James. Oh, Jim, sorry. You have been a teacher at that junior high school for over six years now. The school before that, five. Seems a pattern there Jimmy. You leave before things got out of control? Or, is that about the length of time around you, every day, one needs to spend to sniff you out for your true self? How many kids over eleven years Jim? How many? he paused, solemnly.

"I wonder?" He trailed off, looking away from James Junior the Gym teacher and into the sky that was still starry, but far from the blackness of an hour ago. "I wonder?" He sat there silent for a moment.

"People..." Jim Junior blurted out messily, choking on the word and causing Bob, husband and father, to get out of the stars and back to his friend here in the boat.

He looked at him, mildly interested and flashed one eyebrow as if to say, "uh huh, I'm waiting..."
"People will look for me and when they can't find me, they will come looking for you. You can't kill me without slitting your own throat." He said waiting for a possible hesitation to reason on this awful man's face. All the while twisting his wrists back and forth, over and over, as he had been for every conscious moment since this god forsaken journey began. Stretching his restraints over and over until they loosened enough to wiggle free and knock this smug son of a bitch right into the gulf. He wasn't quite there; he would let this prick talk long enough for him to do what he needed. He was smart. A lot smarter than the dumb gym teacher persona he could put on when he needed. He would keep him talking. Without provocation further,

he did.

"People will miss you Jim. But it will be more of a mystery and less of a whodunit. You know what I am saying to you muchacho? I bought you a cross-country bus ticket, online with your card and your name. You got a good deal. It left for Sitka, Alaska at nine p.m. last night. I neatly packed up a bunch of your shit into suitcases and then incinerated all of it. I stripped your car of any identification, including your VIN number and left that quint little vehicle of yours to the street hoods who have already stripped it and redistributed by now. But last and best of all? You Jim. No sign of YOU. No body. No blood? No crime Jimbo."

"But..." he started to speak but was cut off once again.

"Jim, please. No one is going to look for you for long. Everything points to you just continuing your super vacation. You got back and decided, 'I'm never comin back'. Hell, even if someone by the grace of God, comes looking for you, even in that particular situation, the *last* person anybody is going to be looking at is me, buddy boy." And with that, Jim Junior realized, "of course not." The news had said there was no note.

CHAPTER TWELVE:

CONSTITUTION

Bob's wife, Lila, having heard the note read aloud to her in the most heartbreaking voice she had ever heard, watched as her sadness turned into rage.

Bob, still clutching the note angrily in his hands, heard the sounds of sirens approaching. He had forgotten in his desperation, that he had swiped one of the cop cars, fleeing from his own crime scene at a noticeably high rate of speed.

It felt like last year, but this whole horrible ride he was on was only going for less than thirty minutes from start to stop. Cars had been immediately dispatched after him. Not because he took the car or any such notion like that, but of course when your twenty-year veteran who is also you senior ranking officer, highjacks one of your cruisers, something is wrong.

"Honey. The guys are going to be pulling up on our front lawn in less than sixty seconds." He said matter of fact, still cradling his son.

Lila looked down at the note still in Bob's hand and snatched it back to herself.

"Now, Lila…"he pleaded, "they are gonna want that note. That is evidence." She pulled the note further from his reach and then into her back pocket.

"There was no note." She said calm and collected as the sirens announced their arrival in her front yard with a tire screeching halt.

"Lila, they are going to be up these stairs in no time." He said and now they could both hear the chatter of men exiting cars. But now, she was the calm one.

"No. They don't get him. He doesn't get to have free room and board and three squares a day in club fed for a few years. Our son took his life because he couldn't bear to see him and us dragged through the horror show a trial would bring. And I will be GOD DAMNED if that son of a bitch gets anything less than total misery. We are going to find this son of a bitch and he is going to disappear in the most horrible fashion I can come up with."

"Babe…" he started, but he could see her face was not moving and she would not waiver a tiny bit. Even if he had all the time in the world to debate her and he did not have that.

Back up just slid across the lawn and officers one and two had already entered the house announcing themselves loudly.

"SIR?" one called.

Then the other, "LIEUTENANT ANDERSON?" they inched

forward listening.

"Lieutenant, we are in your house, yell out to us sir, where are you?" Bob Anderson closed his eyes tightly, still holding his little man tight against his chest, thinking, concentrating. Forever had seemed to pass. Those eyes of his stayed slammed shut for only about five seconds before springing back opened again. When they did open, the answer was there. He looked back at his wife, whose gaze had never left his face and yelled out: "We're up here!" He didn't scream, but he was certainly loud enough for all downstairs and outside to hear. Footsteps rapidly ascended stairs as he took the note from her pocket and buried it deep into his own. Lila, cried again softly, not just because she had to but also because it was time again.

The officers reached the top of the stairs, guns drawn, viewing the scene before them, in complete shock. As they looked, they saw their Lieutenant, his wife and their son all huddled on his bedroom floor, evidence of the events that had recently taken place, strewn about the scene.

"Jesus Christ" one managed as they all lowered their weapons slowly. One officer, Dave Pendleton, cried into his hand and turned around and walked right back out.

"Lieutenant, Missus Anderson, I am so sorry, what...what can we do?"

To which he replied, "Nothing. There is nothing."

"Sir, do you want us to call the guys in? Do you want a coroner?"

"No." he said softly, never taking his eyes off of his son. "We'll take him in."

They all sat there for a few more minutes, sitting in silence. Then Bob got up and walked his son to his bed and gently laid him down. He wrapped him in his bed sheets, picked him back up and walked him out of his room for the last time. On his way to the car before heading to the hospital, he thought of the things that were to be officially over from this point on, over for him, over for Lila and most of all, over for their son Brian.

There were questions to be asked and answers would be given, but he was a top dog. A very well respected top dog and with the obviousness of what had happened, it would be quick and easy. Fortunately, the one piece of uneraserable evidence that could be gotten from the cell phone company with ease, the voicemail his son had left him apologizing for what was to come. How he loved him and his mother. Thankfully he said that and only that. But he wouldn't worry about any of that yet. Tonight was for his wife and his boy, tomorrow, he would work out the rest.

CHAPTER THIRTEEN:

FIN

Detective Bob, Robert Anderson, stared at his catch and his catch stared right back at him. Jim Junior knew this was it. He had exhausted his attempts at wringing his hands free and the knife ended up being nothing more than a pipe dream. He knew this man meant to kill him and he felt like that time was upon him. All he thought he might be able to do is convince the man to be humane.

"Please, Mister Anderson, don't drown me please, anything but that. Cut my throat, stab me in the heart and throw me in after I am dead. Please, please don't drown me." He calmly pleaded making his face and eyes as accessible as they had ever been.

The man turned around and walked back towards his seat at the back of the boat. He stopped by the engine and grabbed a life vest. As he walked back towards Jim Junior, Jim no longer looked simply terrified. He had added a rather large helping of confusion to his plate as well. He threw the life vest over the gym teachers' head, taking the threads near the top and tying them tightly around his neck. Not enough to cut off his circulation as Jim Junior initially thought.

He quickly dismissed that sweet lullaby knowing he wasn't getting off with anything as light as asphyxiation.
"What...what the hell are you..."
"Doing? I know, seems a little backwards throwing a man into the deep open ocean to drown and attaching a life jacket to his head to keep him afloat. But... I never said anything to you about drowning, Jim. As terrified at the prospect of drowning seems to make you, brings warmth to my heart, I made a promise to my wife Lila that you would go a certain way. Generally, screaming bloody murder, not to put too fine a point on it. And drowning, while no day at the beach, if you'll pardon the expression, would feel too quick for our tastes. I mean, you could take a mental vacation during your last moments and pretend you were doing something else altogether, maybe something mildly pleasant, even. We just can't have that my not so good sir. We wouldn't want you to be absent for your own main event, now would we?"

Bob took the note back from Jim Junior's lap and held it up to the Gym teachers face before stuffing it down the front of his shirt.
He reached behind him and grabbed the medium sized white fishing bucket that had been silently riding beneath him, unnoticed the whole entire ride and slid it front and center.

"So, …Jim." he paused before quickly resuming.

"Can I call you Jim? I feel at this point, I can. Yeah? Cool?" he continued, not really asking for permission.

"So, as I was saying, I've been coming out here to this very spot, every morning at this precise moment for the last two weeks or so, chumming these waters and then I feed those that show up, with a live gutted pig, just a kicking and screaming."

The look of absolute terror was unmissable now, if it ever had been before.

"Can you hear the splashing?" he paused for effect.

And to Jim Junior's horror, he could.

"Oh God" he thought that was the tide, but oh god, no, it wasn't and he could hear it now.

"Jesus Christ, no!" he cried.

Bob Anderson went on as if he had never stopped speaking.

"If you're not paying precise attention, all of that splashing sounds just like waves slapping up against the hull, doesn't it? But you know better now, don't you Jim?"

Bob Anderson spun that bucket around and got a good grip on the lid that was ever so tight around it and peeled it back revealing a small pool of blood guts and entrails of fish and squid. He lifted the bucket with both hands and held it just above Jim Junior's head.

"NO PLEASE NO!" he screamed in horror.

"No body Jimbo, no crime right?"

He spoke plainly as he dumped the bucket of parts and blood and guts and nasty oils that don't just wash off, the kind that attracts the sort of company he had hoped for this morning. Company, which did not disappoint. He moved the bucket all over the teacher's head and body and near the very end made sure to pour some of it down the front of his shirt with the note, waiting inside. Then, just then, at his finest moment, he grabbed James Flannigan Junior by the back of his shirt and the base of his pants and threw him right over the side as high and hard as he could to generate the largest splash possible.

Jim Junior flew beautifully through the air in slow motion. He could see everything. He sailed for a brief moment, high above the surface to see large torpedo shaped bodies toppling over one another, just underneath, waiting for their score to arrive. They had dined on pig for two weeks straight, but this particular morning, they were about to get a taste of some nice prime rib.

As he descended, the sunlight lay down on the surface of the ocean and brought just enough cover to allow him to make eye contact with the nasty bull shark he was about to land on, covered in chum.

He screamed all the way in and he landed with a loud splash. He submerged for a brief moment, but sure enough the handy dandy life vest did it's job and pulled him right back to the surface, keeping nothing but his head above water. Bob Anderson took this last little moment to tap out the last remaining remnants of the chum bucket over Jim Junior's head. Fins and tails splashed and swam in and around what was to be Jim Junior's final resting places. The float? Still doing a bang up job at keeping him at the surface.

Jim let out a short shriek of pain as one of the smaller sharks came up and took a Nerf football size chunk out of his left love handle. And once fresh blood had been spilled, they came in, one, two, three at a time, ripping off their fair share and moving over for the rest. He flailed uselessly, hands and feet still bound, screaming a mix of blood and ocean.

Brian's father stood tall and smiled. He drew in a tremendous breath and screamed at the top of his lungs, so James Flannigan Junior, could hear him above all of the incessant splashing and screaming.

"THAT'S FOR MY SON, YOU SON OF A BITCH!" He hurled it with all that he had.

He stayed watching for another couple of seconds as Jim Junior was tugged screaming in this direction, then that. Briefly pulled under as they took their choice cuts only to resurface again, coughing, choking, out of breath and being eaten alive.

He then turned to the engine, started the motor and made a big circle around the man who was in the ocean being picked apart like a boar on a spit at a barbeque and then headed back towards home, in the direction he came.

As he got further and further away, the screams seemed to get louder and louder, more and more shrill and full of agony. This pleased him and made him smile all the more, knowing how he would regale his loving wife Lila with the details later on. This brought an even bigger smile to his face.

Soon the screaming was replaced by the gurgling of ocean water. His head was consumed in one final bite, along with the life vest and everything else that was left, by something truly big.

It brought Bob comfort to know that Jim Junior's last seven to ten minutes of brain activity would result in an eternity of rolling around the stomach of a very large shark. Hell on earth indeed.

Soon, all that remained was the splashing that was caused by a fight over scraps, which would slowly settle to the ocean floor or float on the surface for some of the smaller fish and birds to get at.

Bob motored home to his wife with the first bits of good news in some time. Satisfied. He powered towards home and as he did the sun began to rise behind him, warming his back and lighting his whole way home.

THE END

January 2013-July 2017

About the Author

Michael Spinelli was born in Queens, New York.
He is married to his loving wife for 14 years and has two equally insane sons.
He currently resides in Florida like his literary idol, Stephen King.

He is NOT quitting his day job.

46018112R00051

Made in the USA
Middletown, DE
24 July 2017